The Good Earth

Pearl S. Buck

Abridged and adapted by Emily Hutchinson

Illustrated by Karen Loccisano

A PACEMAKER CLASSIC

GLOBE FEARON
EDUCATIONAL PUBLISHER
PARAMUS, NEW JERSEY

Paramount Publishing

Supervising Editor: Stephen Feinstein
Project Editor: Karen Bernhaut
Editorial Assistant: Stacie Dozier
Art Director: Nancy Sharkey
Assistant Art Director: Armando Baéz
Production Manager: Penny Gibson
Production Editor: Nicole Cypher
Desktop Specialist: Eric Dawson
Manufacturing Supervisor: Della Smith
Marketing Manager: Marge Curson
Cover Illustration: Karen Loccisano

Printed in the United States of America
1 2 3 4 5 6 7 8 9 10 99 98 97 96 95 94

ISBN 0–835–91059–8

GLOBE FEARON
EDUCATIONAL PUBLISHER
PARAMUS, NEW JERSEY

Paramount Publishing

Contents

Cast of Characters

Wang Lung — A Chinese farmer who rises to become the head of a powerful house

Wang Lung's father — An elderly man who lives with Wang Lung until he dies

O-lan — A former slave who becomes the wife of Wang Lung and helps him build his fortune

Wang Lung's uncle — A lazy and evil man who demands support from Wang Lung

Wang Lung's eldest son (Nun En) — Sent to school, in part so he can read and write for Wang Lung

Wang Lung's second son (Nun Wen) — Also given an education and later becomes a grain merchant

Wang Lung's third son — A quiet boy who later joins the revolutionary army

Wang Lung's eldest daugher ("poor fool") — A child who does not develop mentally

Ching — A neighboring farmer and trusted overseer of Wang Lung's lands

Lotus — A beautiful young girl who Wang Lung falls in love with and takes into his house

Cuckoo — A former slave in the House of Hwang who later works as a servant to Lotus

Pear Blossom — A young slave bought by Wang Lung who becomes his devoted companion

1 Wang Lung's Marriage

It was Wang Lung's wedding day. As he woke, he heard his father coughing. Every morning, this was the first sound Wang Lung heard. Through the small open window, he could see the morning sky.

He felt a soft wind blowing from the east. The wind seemed full of the promise of rain. It was a good sign. The fields needed rain so the crops could grow. Now it was as if Heaven had chosen this day to wish him well. Earth would bear fruit.

He hurried out into the middle room, pulling on his trousers as he went. He went into the kitchen, a shed that leaned against the house. Both kitchen and house were made of earthen bricks dug from Wang Lung's fields. The rooms were thatched with straw made from Wang Lung's wheat.

Wang Lung began to put water into the deep, round, iron pot that was on top of the oven. He dipped it from an earthen jar that stood nearby. Water was precious, so he dipped it carefully. Then he suddenly lifted the jar and emptied all the water into the pot. This day he would bathe his whole body. It was a special day, and he wanted to be clean.

He put some straw into the oven and lit it. This was the last morning he would have to light the fire. He had lit it every morning since his mother died six years before. Now he could rest. A woman was coming to the house. Never again would Wang Lung have to rise at dawn to light the fire.

If the woman got tired, there would be the children to light the fire. For Wang Lung was sure that she would bear him many children. Wang Lung thought of the three rooms full of children. The fire in the oven died down while Wang Lung thought of all the beds they would have. The old man appeared in the doorway, coughing and spitting. He gasped, "Where is the hot water to heat my lungs?"

The old man kept on coughing until the water heated again. Wang Lung dipped some into a bowl. Then he put some tea leaves on the surface of the water. "Why are you wasting the tea? Wasting tea is like eating silver," complained the old man.

"It is a special day," said Wang Lung with a laugh. "Drink the tea and be happy."

The old man began to take great gulps of the hot tea. Then he noticed that Wang Lung was dipping the water into a deep wooden tub. He stared at his son and said, "That is enough water for a field of crops!"

"I have not washed my body all at once since the New Year," said Wang Lung in a low voice. He was ashamed to say to his father that he wanted to be clean for his new wife.

"It is not good for the woman to get used to this—tea in the morning and all this washing!" said the old man.

"It is only one day," said Wang Lung. "I will throw the water on the earth when I'm done. I won't waste it."

The old man was silent as Wang Lung took his bath. Then Wang Lung put on a fresh suit of blue cotton cloth. He put on his one long robe, which he wore on feast days only, ten days or so a year. Then he undid his long braid and began to comb out his hair. His father came to the door again and said, "Am I to have nothing to eat this day?"

"I am coming," said Wang Lung, braiding his hair quickly. He took off his long robe, wound his braid about his head, and went out, carrying the tub of water. He poured the water on the earth and fixed his father's breakfast. Then he put on the long robe again and let down his braid.

Before leaving the house, he counted his money. He had not yet told his father that he had invited his cousin, his uncle, and three neighboring farmers to share a special wedding dinner that night. He hoped he would have enough money to buy the food and get a shave as well.

He went out into the early morning, walking on the narrow path. In the near distance the gray city wall arose. Inside the gate stood the great house where the woman lived. The only thing Wang Lung knew about her was that she was not pretty.

When he had first heard this, he was disappointed. But his father had said, "What would we do with a pretty woman? We must have a woman who will keep house, bear children, and work in the fields. Would a pretty woman do these things?"

Wang Lung knew that his father was right about the kind of woman they needed. And today was the day Wang Lung could go and get her.

He walked into the city and soon was on the Street of Barbers. He went to one of them and sat down on a stool. The barber began to pour hot water from a kettle into a brass basin. "Shave everything?" he asked in a professional tone.

"My head and my face," said Wang Lung.

"The new style is to cut off the braid," said the barber.

"I cannot cut it off without asking my father!" said Wang Lung. So the barber shaved off all but the round spot of hair. Now Wang Lung was ready to meet his new wife. On the way to the great house, he bought some pork, beef, and fish for the wedding feast. He also bought a pair of incense sticks. When he got to the great house, he felt very nervous. The gateman at the house, who was polite only to rich people, was rude to Wang Lung. He even demanded money before he would let him in.

Finally, after passing through many rooms, Wang Lung was led to a large room. There he saw an old woman sitting on a raised platform. Beside her was an opium pipe, which she smoked from time to time. Her eyes were small, sharp, and sunken in her thin and wrinkled face. "Have you come for the slave called O-lan?" she asked. "I remember we promised her to some farmer. Are you that farmer?"

"Yes, I am," replied Wang Lung.

"Call O-lan quickly," said the old woman to her slave. Moments later, the slave returned leading a square, rather tall figure. The woman was dressed in a clean blue cotton coat and trousers. Wang Lung glanced at her quickly, his heart beating.

"This man has come for you," said the old woman. "Are you ready?"

The woman answered slowly as an echo, "Ready."

Wang Lung liked her voice. It was not too loud or too soft. It was plain and pleasant. Her hair was neat and smooth, and her clothes were clean. He saw with disappointment that her feet were not bound. But he could not think about that, for the old woman was speaking to him.

She said, "O-lan has been here for ten years, since she was ten years old. I bought her in a year of famine, when her parents had nothing to eat. You see that she is strong. She is not beautiful, and she is not very smart. But she will do what she is told." Then to the woman, she said, "Obey him and bear him many sons. Bring the first child to me to see."

Then Wang Lung and O-lan left. When he turned to look at her, he could see that she was not pretty. But she was not ugly, either. She had a square, honest face, and he was pleased with her.

As they walked back to his house, O-lan followed six paces behind Wang Lung. They stopped at the western field, at the small temple that Wang Lung's grandfather had built. Inside the temple were two small earthen figures—the earth god and his lady. Together, Wang Lung and O-lan stood before the gods of their fields. They lit the incense that Wang Lung had bought earlier. They stood there in complete silence, side by side, as the incense burned. This was the moment of their marriage. Then they picked up the food Wang Lung had bought and went home.

When they got there, Wang Lung said, "There are seven people to feed. Can you prepare this food?"

"I have been a kitchen slave for the past ten years," she said. "I cooked for every meal."

Later, Wang Lung asked her to serve the dinner. She said, "I will hand you the bowls if you will put them on the table. I do not like to come out before men."

Wang Lung was proud of his wife's modesty, just as he was proud of her cooking. That night, when they were alone, he felt shy at first. But when she came to bed, he was filled with happiness.

The next morning he watched the woman rise from his bed as though she had risen from it every day of her life. "Take my father some hot water for his lungs," he said. And then he lay in his bed, warm and happy, while she started the fire and boiled the water. Suddenly, he wanted her to like him as her husband, and then he was ashamed. But when she brought him some tea in bed, he was pleased. "This woman of mine likes me well enough!" he thought to himself.

Over the next few months, O-lan worked hard. She kept the house clean, cooked the meals, mended the old clothes, and helped Wang Lung in the fields. She also went out and gathered grass, twigs, and leaves for fuel. It pleased Wang Lung that they didn't have to buy fuel any longer. One day, she told Wang Lung that she was expecting a child. He was happy and proud.

As the day of the birth came near, Wang Lung said, "We must get a woman to help. We will ask someone from the great house."

"No!" said the woman. "When I return to that house, it will be with my son in my arms. He will be wearing a red coat, red-flowered trousers, a red hat, and tiger-faced shoes. And I will wear new shoes and a new black satin coat. I will show myself and my son to all of them!" Wang Lung was surprised to find out that she had such a plan. He gave her three pieces of silver so she could buy the cloth for the new clothing.

Later, he sat thinking of the silver. Before, when he had given silver to anyone, it had been like taking a piece of his life and giving it away. But this time, such giving was not pain. He saw the silver changed into something worth more than itself—clothes for his son.

When the time came, O-lan would have no one with her. She wouldn't even let Wang Lung into the room. He could hear her loud panting, like whispered screams, but she made no other sound. When he could stand it no longer and was about to break into the room, he heard a fierce cry. "Is it a boy?" he asked, forgetting to ask how O-lan was.

She answered, as faintly as an echo, "A boy."

"I suppose we shall have no more peace in this house now," he said to himself proudly. Later, O-lan called him into the room. She was lying on the bed. Beside her, wrapped warmly, lay his son.

For a moment he could hardly speak, he was so happy. His heart rushed out to the two of them. Finally, he said, "Tomorrow I will buy a basket full of eggs and dye them all red for the village. Then everyone will know I have a son!"

2 Changes in Fortune

The day after the child was born, Wang Lung bought 50 eggs and some red dye. He also bought a pound of red sugar for O-lan. The sugar dealer asked, smiling, "Is it for the mother of a newborn child, perhaps?"

"A first-born son," said Wang Lung proudly.

"Ah, good fortune," said the man. The sugar dealer said this every day to someone, but to Wang Lung it seemed special. He felt that there was never a man as lucky as he.

But then he felt a pang of fear. It was not good in this life to be too fortunate. There were spirits who did not like it if poor people were too happy. For protection, he bought four sticks of incense, one for each person in his house. He burned these at the temple of the gods of the earth. Then he went home, feeling better.

Soon O-lan was back in the fields, working by Wang Lung's side. She worked all day, as the child lay asleep on an old torn quilt on the ground. When he cried, the woman stopped her work to nurse him. She had more than enough milk for the child, greedy though he was. The child was fat and happy.

When winter came, they had plenty of food. They had dried onions and garlic. There were great jars filled with wheat and rice. There was dried meat hanging from the rafters. Wang Lung had saved this food to sell when the snow fell. He would sell when people in the towns would pay well for food.

When the child was one month old, they had a feast of noodles, which mean long life. Everyone in the village envied Wang Lung because of his great, fat son with high cheekbones. "There is not another child like this in a dozen villages," thought Wang Lung. "He is smarter than any of the children of my brother."

Wang Lung's home was filled with more warmth and plenty than any other in the village. He and O-lan worked hard and were happy with each other. If an earthen jar leaked, O-lan did not throw it out as other wives did. Instead she would mix earth and clay and repair the jar.

By the end of the year, Wang Lung had more silver pieces than he needed. He hid the silver in a small hole dug in the wall behind their bed. O-lan covered the hole with a clod of earth, and it looked as if nothing was there. But to Wang Lung and O-lan, it gave a feeling of secret richness.

On the second day of the New Year, Wang Lung and O-lan rose at dawn. O-lan dressed the child in the red coat, hat, and tiger-faced shoes she had made. Then Wang Lung and O-lan put on their new black coats. Carrying the child and some colorful New Year's cakes that O-lan had made, they set out for the House of Hwang.

The gateman showed a new respect for Wang Lung. As he looked at the new clothes and the healthy baby, he said, "Sit in my room. I will announce your wife and child in the inner courts." As Wang Lung waited, he was served tea by the gateman's wife. But he did not drink it, acting as if the quality of the tea were not good enough for him.

When O-lan and the baby finally returned, Wang Lung could see that she had something to tell him. On their way back home, Wang Lung looked over his shoulder as she followed him. "Well?" he asked.

She came up closer and whispered, "Money must be tight in the great house this year. The Old Mistress was wearing last year's coat. None of the slaves had a new coat like mine. As for our son, there was not a single child in there as beautiful or as well-dressed." A slow smile spread across her face. Wang Lung laughed aloud.

"Did you find out why they are poorer?" he asked.

"I had only a minute to talk to the cook. She told me that the young lords in the house are

spending money like water. And the Old Mistress is using a lot of opium. They must sell some of their land because they need the money."

"Sell their land!" said Wang Lung. "Then indeed they are growing poor. Land is one's life." Then a thought suddenly came to him. "We will buy it!"

"It is a good thing to buy land," said O-lan. "It is better than putting money into a mud wall."

And again a slow smile spread over O-lan's face. She would be the wife of a man who owned a piece of the land that had made the House of Hwang great. After a long time she said, "Last year at this time I was a slave in that house." And they walked on, silently thinking about this.

The land that Wang Lung bought changed his life. It was more than a third of a mile from his home. And it needed a lot of work to make it suitable for planting. He worked long hours each day, with O-lan at his side. When Wang Lung noticed one day that again O-lan was with child, he was annoyed. He could only think that during the harvest she would be unable to work.

One autumn morning, she put down her hoe and crept into the house. Wang Lung did not even go home for the noon meal, for the rice was ripe for gathering. Later that day, before the sun set, she was back beside him. He thought about saying, "For this day you have done enough." But instead, he said, "Is it male or female?"

She answered calmly, "It is another male." They said nothing more, but he was pleased. They worked side by side until the moon rose, and then they went home. When Wang Lung had eaten his meal and washed up, he went in to see his second son. As he looked at the baby, he thought to himself that this woman brought him nothing but good fortune.

That year, the harvests were good. The new land was wet and rich, and the rice grew on it as weeds grow where they are not wanted. Everyone knew now that Wang Lung owned this land. In the village, there was talk of making him the head.

At this time Wang Lung's uncle began to make trouble for Wang Lung. According to custom, this uncle could depend on Wang Lung if he didn't have enough for himself and his family. As long as Wang Lung was poor, the uncle did what he could to feed his own family. But now Wang Lung was doing well.

One day the uncle came to Wang Lung in the fields. O-lan was not there, for ten months had passed since the birth of their second child. A third birth was close upon her, and for a few days she had not felt well. As soon as Wang Lung saw his uncle, he knew that he had come to ask for something. The uncle soon got to the point.

"I have always had bad luck. No matter what I do, the beans in my field do not grow. And my wife does nothing but get fatter and give birth to females. That one lazy son of mine is no help to me. My eldest daughter is 15, as you know. It is time she is married. But I have no money to pay a matchmaker to find her a husband. If you give me ten pieces of silver, I could pay the matchmaker. You know that this is your duty. If you refuse, I will tell the whole village that you have no respect for your elders," said the uncle.

So Wang Lung put down his hoe and went to the house. He was angry because he knew that his uncle would use the money to gamble. As he walked into the bedroom to get the silver, he saw his wife. She was holding the baby that had just been born. "It is only a girl this time," she said weakly.

Wang Lung stood still. A sense of evil struck him. A girl! It seemed that Wang Lung's luck was changing. Not only did he have to give silver to his uncle, but now he had a daughter.

After the uncle left, Wang Lung went back out into the field to continue working. It was evening before he got over his anger. He thought of the new mouth that had come into his house that day. He thought about the fact that daughters do not belong to their parents. They are born and reared for other families. Across the pale sky, a flock of crows flew, cawing loudly. He groaned aloud. It was a bad sign.

3 Days of Drought

The rains that should have fallen in early summer did not come. Most of the fields that Wang Lung had planted grew dry and cracked. Only the piece of land that had once belonged to the House of Hwang bore any harvest. This was because Wang Lung spent his days dipping water from the nearby moat to pour on that soil. This year for the first time, he sold his grain as soon as it was harvested. As soon as he had the silver in his hand, he went back to the House of Hwang.

When he said to the land agent, "I have silver," it was as if he were saying to the hungry, "I have food." For the House of Hwang had almost run out of money. The papers were signed quickly. This time Wang Lung didn't even tell O-lan that he had spent their money on more land.

Months passed, and still no rain fell. From his fields, Wang Lung had very small harvests of beans and corn. When he started to put the corn cobs away for fuel, O-lan said, "No. Do not waste them in burning. I remember when I was a child, we even ground and ate the cobs. It is better than grass."

The only one in the family who had no fear was the baby girl. That was because her mother had plenty of milk for her. But soon O-lan was again with child, and her milk dried up. The house was filled with the cries of a hungry child.

One day, Wang Lung's father said, "We will eat the ox next." To Wang Lung, that was like saying, "We will eat a man next." The ox had been his companion in the fields since it had been a calf.

Wang Lung said, "How can we eat the ox? How would we plow again?"

The old man answered, "It's your life or the ox's. You can always buy another ox, but you can't buy your life back."

Wang Lung agreed, but he could not kill the animal. He told O-lan to do it, and she did. The meat fed the family for a time, but it was soon gone. When the uncle came to Wang Lung for food to feed his family, Wang Lung had nothing to give.

The uncle began talking about Wang Lung in the village. He said that Wang Lung was hiding food and silver in his house. By this time, everyone in the village was starving. One night, the men broke down Wang Lung's door. When they found only a few dried beans and some dried corn, they became angry. They started to seize the furniture.

O-lan came forward and spoke to them. "Heaven will strike you if you take any more.

19

Tomorrow we will go out together and hunt for grass to eat. You will search for food for your children. And we will search for food for our three children, and for this fourth who will soon be born." The men were ashamed and left, for they were not evil men except when they starved.

One man, Ching, would have said he was sorry, for he was an honest man. He had stolen a few beans for his crying child. He was afraid that if he spoke, he would have to return them. So he only looked at Wang Lung with sad eyes and went out.

Wang Lung stood in his yard. There was nothing left in the house to feed his family. Then he thought, "They cannot take the land from me. If I had the silver, they would have taken it. If I had bought food with the silver, they would have taken it all. I have the land still, and it is mine."

As the days went by, his family became weaker and weaker. They barely got out of bed now. There was no need, and fitful sleep took the place of food. They had eaten the cobs of corn, and they had stripped the bark from trees.

Wang Lung's two sons were thin, with their sharp small bones sticking out like the bones of birds. The girl never even sat up, although she was old enough to do so. She lay quietly hour after hour wrapped in an old quilt. Her little hollow face peered out at them all.

In some way, the little girl began to win her father's affection. If she had been as round and merry as the others had been at her age, he might not have noticed her. Sometimes, looking at her, he whispered, "Poor fool, poor little fool."

One day, Wang Lung declared, "We will leave this place. We will go south! People are not starving everywhere in this great land."

O-lan said, "You are right. We will leave tomorrow. I shall have given birth by then."

When Wang Lung saw how weak his wife looked, he was moved to pity. "How shall you walk, you poor creature?" he muttered to himself. He went to his neighbor, Ching, and said, "If you have any food left, please help me. It would save the life of the mother of my sons. If you help me, I will forget that I saw you in my house as a robber."

Ching looked at him ashamed and said, "I have never thought of you with peace since that hour. I felt terrible about what happened. I have only a handful of beans, but I will give some to you."

Ching brought two handfuls of red beans to Wang Lung. He took the food to his wife, and she ate a little. She knew that if she didn't, she would die in the pain of giving birth. Wang Lung saved a few of the beans and chewed them to a pulp.

Then he pushed the pulp into the mouth of his daughter. In watching her small lips move, he felt himself fed.

That night, O-lan again gave birth alone. He listened for the little cry he knew so well. Male or female, it didn't matter to him now. There was only another mouth coming, which must be fed. Then he heard the weak cry hanging for an instant in the stillness. There was no second cry. Suddenly Wang Lung was afraid. He went to the door of the room where O-lan lay and said, "Are you safe?" Suppose she had died as he sat there! But he heard movement, and then she said, "Come in!"

He went in and saw the child on the floor.

"Dead!" he exclaimed.

"Dead," she whispered.

He bent down and looked at the body—a wisp of bone and skin—a girl. He said nothing, and he took the dead child into the other room. The round head dropped this way and that. Upon the neck he saw two dark, bruised spots. He wrapped the body in a roll of matting, took it outside, and buried it.

The next day, his thought of traveling to the South seemed impossible. How could his helpless children, his weakened wife, and his old father drag themselves hundreds of miles? They weren't even sure that there was food in the South. Perhaps they would get there only to find more starving people. Maybe they'd be better off dying in their own beds.

He had no money. But even if he did, there was no food to be bought. As he thought about all this, he saw some men coming across the fields toward him. As they got closer, he saw that it was his uncle and three other men. He could tell that his uncle had been eating. He was thin, it was true, but not starving. Wang Lung remembered the rumors he had heard that some people had been eating human flesh.

The uncle and the other men had come to offer to buy Wang Lung's land. They offered him one-twentieth of what he had paid. They were sure that because his family was starving, he would take it. Wang Lung's anger was greater than he had ever known. "I shall never sell the land!" he shrieked at them.

O-lan backed him up. "If we sell the land, we would have nothing when we return from the South. Nor will we sell the rakes, the hoe, or the plow. But we will sell the furniture and even the pot on the stove."

The men gave them two pieces of silver—less than the cost of one bed—for all the furniture. Wang Lung used most of that money to pay for train fare. Until that day, he had only heard about the "firewagons." Now his family would travel on a machine that breathed forth fire and water like a dragon.

4 Hard Times

After buying the train tickets, Wang Lung had a handful of pennies left. He used a few of these to buy some bread and rice for his family. He saved the rest to buy some mats when they got to the South. He would bind six mats together to make a hut to shelter the family. A man on the train gave Wang Lung some tips about what to do once they got to the city.

"You must go out and beg," the man said. "But first smear yourself and your family with mud so you'll look really piteous. People will feel sorry for you and give you some money."

Wang Lung had never in his life begged, and he didn't like the idea. "One must beg?" he asked.

"Yes, indeed," said the man. "But not until you eat. The people in the South have so much rice that each morning you may go to a public kitchen and for a penny eat as much as you can. Then you can beg comfortably and buy better food later."

Wang Lung counted his money. There was enough for the six mats and one serving of rice each. Beyond that he had three cents. He had a feeling of comfort that they could begin a new life. But the idea of begging still didn't appeal to him. It would be fine for the old man and for the children and even for the woman, but he had his two hands.

"Is there no work for a man to do?" he asked.

"You can pull a rich man in a yellow riksha. It is very hard work. I'd rather beg!" said the man.

When they got to the city, Wang Lung went off to buy the mats. When he returned, he could see that his sons had been filled with terror in this strange place. Every now and then, a caravan of donkeys came by, carrying baskets of bricks and grain. At the end of each caravan, a driver rode on the last animal. He would crack a big whip to keep the donkeys moving. These drivers seemed to enjoy cracking their whips just as they passed the frightened children. Wang Lung looked for someplace else to put his hut.

He saw a long high wall. Against the base, many small mat sheds clung like fleas to a dog's back. Wang Lung tried to put his hut together as the others were put together, but he was having a hard time. Suddenly O-lan said, "I can do that. I remember it from my childhood."

Soon she had shaped a rounded roof high enough for a man to sit under and not hit the top. On the edges of the mats that were on the ground, she placed some bricks. As the family sat in their little shelter, it seemed to Wang Lung that they were lucky to be there.

The next thing they did was find the public kitchens they had heard about. For a penny each, they were filled and had some food left over. Wang Lung wanted to bring the extra back to their hut, but a guard stopped him. "You can take only what is in your belly," he said.

"Well, if I have paid my penny, what do you care if I carry it inside or outside of me?"

"A penny does not pay the cost of the food. The food is paid for by the rich people in the town. There are some people who would take this rice home for their pigs. But the food is for people, not for pigs, and you must eat it here."

Then Wang Lung and his family went to their hut and slept till the next morning. It was the first time since summer that they had been filled with food. The next day, Wang Lung knew that they had to do something to get money. He looked at O-lan, with doubt about what should be done. But it was not with the same despair he had felt at home. Here, at least, there was plenty of food. A man and his family surely would not starve.

O-lan had begged as a child before she was sold as a slave. Now she taught her children how to do it.

As for Wang Lung, he found a place where rikshas were for hire. For the price of some silver to be paid at night, he took one. He dragged it after him out onto the street. As he pulled the rickety, wooden wagon on its two wheels, he felt like a fool. He was as awkward as an ox yoked for the first time to the plow. He could hardly walk, yet he must run if he was to earn a living.

Just as he was thinking that he'd be better off begging, a door opened. An old man who looked like a teacher stepped out and called to him. The old man said, "Take me to the Confucian temple." Wang Lung started out, even though he had no idea where the Confucian temple was. He asked people as he went along, and by the time he got there he was sore and aching. Then the old man got out and gave him a silver coin, saying, "I never pay any more than this. So there is no use in complaining."

Wang Lung had no thought of complaining, since he had never seen such a coin before. He had no idea what it was worth. He had it changed into copper at a nearby shop, and he received 26 cents. Another riksha puller leaned over and said, "Only 26! How far did you pull that old man?" When Wang Lung told him, the other riksha puller said, "He gave you only half the usual fare. What did you argue for before you started?"

"I did not argue," said Wang Lung.

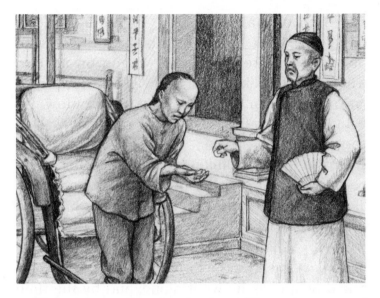

The other man looked at Wang Lung and laughed. "You are obviously from the country, with your pigtail and all! You'd better learn to set a price before you carry someone!"

Wang Lung said nothing. All he could think was that the money would feed his family tomorrow. But then he remembered that he still had to pay for the riksha that night. He did not have even half the money he needed for that.

He had three more passengers that day, and he agreed on prices first. But at night, when he paid for the riksha, he had only one penny left over. He walked back to his hut sadly, thinking about better days at home. The thought of his land lying there, waiting for him, filled him with longing.

When he got to the hut, he found that O-lan and the boys had earned enough to pay for rice in the morning. But the old man had not done anything. He knew that his son and his grandsons would take care of him, for that was the custom.

As time passed, Wang Lung learned more about the city where he was now living. But he lived in this city as a rat in a rich man's house. Fed on the scraps that were thrown away, he never really felt a part of that house. To make matters worse, he could barely understand the language spoken there.

In Anhwei, where Wang Lung was born, the language was slow and deep, and it flowed from the throat. But in the Kiangsu city where they now lived, the accent was different. The people here spoke in syllables that splintered from their lips and from the ends of their tongues. The language here could be understood only with difficulty.

One day, Wang Lung heard a young man giving a speech in front of the Confucian temple. He said that China must have a revolution and must rise against the hated foreigners. Another day he heard another young man saying that the people of China must unite and must educate themselves. It did not occur to Wang Lung that anyone was speaking to him.

As time went by, Wang Lung noticed that there was no shortage of food in the city. At the fish markets big fish, small fish, crabs, and eels filled the vendors' baskets. The grain markets were full of wheat and beans of all kinds and colors. The meat markets were full of hogs, ducks, geese, pheasants, and every kind of fowl. As for vegetables, there was everything that grew in the soil. There were red and white radishes, green cabbages and celery, bean sprouts, and more. There were also sweets, fruits, nuts, and cakes.

Still, all Wang Lung and his family could afford was the bowl of rice at the kitchens for the poor. They could not even buy enough rice to cook at home. One night he came home late and there was a stew of cabbage and pork cooking. It was the first time they had meat to eat since they had killed their own ox. When his younger son bragged that he had stolen the meat, Wang Lung refused to eat it.

"We will eat meat that we can buy or beg for, but not that we steal. Beggars we may be, but thieves we are not," he said. He knew then that they had to get back to the land.

"If I had anything to sell, I would sell it and go back to the land. If it weren't for my father, our daughter, and your condition, we could walk," he said to O-lan.

O-lan, who by now was expecting another child, said, "There is nothing to sell except the girl."

Wang Lung caught his breath. "I would never sell a child!" he said loudly.

"I was sold," she answered. "I was sold to a great house so that my parents could return to their home."

"And would you sell your daughter?" he asked.

"If I were alone, she would be killed before she was sold. But a dead girl brings nothing. I would sell this girl for you—to take you back to the land."

"Never!" said Wang Lung.

He looked at the little girl, playing with her grandfather. She had grown on the food given to her each day. Although she had not started talking yet, she was becoming as plump as a child should be. Lately, whenever he looked at her, she smiled at him. "I might have done it," he thought, "if she hadn't started smiling at me like that."

5 Better Times

As spring came to the village of huts, Wang Lung felt more and more like an outsider. Most of the ragged men had nothing but what they got each day. But Wang Lung owned land, and his land was waiting for him. He belonged to the land, and he would not be happy until he got back to it.

These ragged men in the huts talked always of money. They discussed what they had paid for a foot of cloth or a small fish. They talked of what they could earn in a day. Every day the talk ended with what they would do if they had more money.

They talked about how much they would eat and sleep. They talked about how they would gamble in the great tea shop. And they talked about how they would never work again.

Then Wang Lung cried out suddenly, "If I had money, I would buy good land with it. I would bring forth harvests from the land!"

They said, "Here is a pig-tailed man from the country who knows nothing about the city. He would keep on working like a slave behind an ox!" They thought they were better than Wang

Lung because they would know better how to spend money. But this did not change Wang Lung's mind. Each day, he grew more impatient to be back on his own land.

Then Wang Lung saw something new that he did not understand. As he was pulling his riksha, looking for a customer, he saw a man seized by soldiers. When the man protested, the soldiers held knives to his face. Wang Lung saw many men taken in this way. He realized that they were all common men who worked with their hands. He hid his riksha in an alley and darted into a nearby shop. He asked the old shopkeeper what was happening.

"A war is going on somewhere. Who knows what the fighting is for? But the soldiers need men to carry their guns, ammunition, and other supplies. So they force laborers like you to do it. The only pay is a little bit of food each day. You may go home when the soldiers get where they are going, if your two legs can carry you," said the old man.

"But a man's family—" said Wang Lung, shocked.

"What do they care about that?" said the old man. "Now, get down. Here they come again." And Wang Lung hid as the soldiers clattered down the street. When they were gone, Wang Lung ran to his hut, pulling his riksha behind him.

He told O-lan what had happened. As he spoke, he felt a great fear of being dragged to battlefields, leaving his family alone to starve. And he pictured himself dying on a battlefield, never again to see his own land. "Now I am truly tempted to sell the girl and go north to the land," he said.

O-lan answered, "Wait a few days. There is strange talk going around."

From that day on, Wang Lung did not go out during the daylight. He sent his elder son to return the riksha, and he got another job. For half of what he had earned before, he pulled big wagons full of boxes. It took 12 men to move each wagon. The boxes were filled with silks, cottons, sweet-smelling tobacco, oils, and wines. All night he strained against the ropes that were pulling the wagons. His body streamed with sweat, and his bare feet slipped on the damp streets.

Each day, he got home before dawn, gasping and too tired to eat until he had slept. And during the day when the soldiers searched the streets, he hid in the hut behind a pile of straw.

The city was full of unrest and fear. All day, horse-drawn carriages took rich people to the river. Ships then carried the rich people, their satin-covered bedding, and their jewels away to other places. His sons would come home with stories of the riches they had seen in the city. The elder son said, "We saw many boxes, and I asked what was in them. Someone told me, 'There is gold and silver in them, but the rich cannot take away all they have. Someday it will all be ours.' What did he mean, father?" asked the boy.

When Wang Lung said he did not know, the boy said, "I wish we could go right now and get it. I would like to taste a cake. I have never tasted a sweet cake with sesame seeds on the top."

This talk about sweet cakes made Wang Lung remember the cakes O-lan had made for the New Year's feast. His mouth watered, and his heart ached for those days.

Suddenly it seemed to him that he could not stay in the city one more day. He even thought that his daughter might be better off in the house of a rich family. He thought once more about selling her. But when O-lan described to him how slaves are beaten and mistreated every day, he knew he couldn't do it. He held the child to him and said over and over to her, "Oh, little fool—oh, poor little fool."

Suddenly as he sat there, there was a loud noise outside the hut. Everyone in the family fell to the ground and hid their faces.

Then the noise stopped as suddenly as it had started. O-lan said, "I heard that this was going to happen, but I didn't believe it. The enemy has broken in the gates of the city." Then there was shouting over the city, a rising tide of human voices. This was followed by a deep howl that got louder and louder as it filled the streets.

One of their neighbors stuck his head into their hut and said, "Why are you just sitting there? The hour has come. The gates of the rich man are open to us." Wang Lung and O-lan stepped outside the hut and were quickly swept away in the crowd. Wang Lung found himself being carried into the gates, through court after court, and finally into the great house.

He saw none of the people who had lived in the house. But food was on a table, and the kitchen fires were still burning. The crowd swept through the house and found the treasures inside—the silks, the jewels, and the scrolls. They stole everything, including curtains, dishes, and bedding.

Wang Lung took nothing. He had never in all his life taken what belonged to another. He pushed his way to the edge of the crowd, to get away from the madness.

He found himself at the back of the innermost court, and the back gate was open. That gate, which the rich always keep for their escape in such times, is called the gate of peace. It was through that gate that the rich people had fled.

One man, whether because of his huge size or because he had been sleeping, had failed to escape. Wang Lung came upon this man in an empty inner room, where he had been hiding. Now he was crawling out to escape. When he saw Wang Lung, he shook all over and yelled out, as if he had been stuck with a knife. Wang Lung, who of course had no weapon, almost laughed out loud.

The fat fellow fell upon his knees. "Save a life, do not kill me," he begged. "I have money for you, lots of it."

It was this word "money" that got Wang Lung's attention. The child would be saved. He could go back to his land. "Give me the money, then!" he demanded.

Wang Lung held out the end of his coat, and the man filled it with silver. "Now there is none left, and I have nothing but my wretched life," the fat man cried. The tears were running like oil down his fat cheeks.

Suddenly Wang Lung hated the man as he had hated nothing before. He cried out, "Out of my sight!" The man ran past him like a dog and was gone. Then Wang Lung was left alone with the silver. All he could think was, "Tomorrow we go back to the land."

After a few days had passed, it seemed to Wang Lung that he had never been away from

his land. Indeed, in his heart he never had. He
bought seeds and an ox before he even got
home, so eager was he to begin planting.

When they got home, they found that the door
had been torn away. The thatch from the roof
was gone, and their hoes and rakes had been
stolen. Wang Lung asked his neighbors who had
taken these things. His neighbor Ching told him
that a band of robbers had lived in his house
during the winter. "It is said that your uncle
knows more about them than an honest man
should," said Ching.

Ching then told Wang Lung what a hard winter
it had been. His wife had died, and he had to sell
his daughter to keep her from starving. "If I had

any seeds, I would plant again," said Ching. "But I have nothing."

"Come here!" said Wang Lung, and he gave Ching some seeds. "Tomorrow I will help you plow your land with my good ox." When Ching began to weep, Wang Lung said, "Do you think I forgot that you once gave me a handful of beans?"

Over the next few months, Wang Lung and O-lan were busy putting their house and land back in order. Wang Lung was glad to find out that his uncle was gone from the village. Some said that he, his wife, and his son had gone to a city. The girls had been sold.

Soon, Wang Lung's house was itself again. They had new candlesticks, a new teapot, dishes, and beds. O-lan grew large with the next child, and Wang Lung's father sat and smiled as he dozed. In the fields, the young rice sprouted as green as jade and more beautiful. And they had enough silver to feed themselves until the harvest.

One night, Wang Lung discovered that O-lan had stolen some jewels from the rich man's house. Having lived in a rich man's house before, she knew that there were many hiding places. "I knew the meaning of a loosened brick," she explained.

Wang Lung said, "We cannot keep a treasure like this. It must be sold—into land, for nothing else is safe. If anyone knew about these jewels, we would be robbed."

When O-lan asked to keep two small pearls, Wang Lung was surprised. He thought of this dull and faithful woman, who had worked all her life. He imagined her in the great house, seeing others wearing jewels that she could never touch. Moved by something he did not understand, he gave her the two small pearls.

The next day, he took the jewels to the House of Hwang to see if there was more land to buy. Wang Lung pounded a long time at the door before it was finally answered. There was only one servant, a woman named Cuckoo, left in the house.

Wang Lung did not want to do business with a woman. But she told him that she and the Old Lord were the only ones there. She explained that bandits had come into the house. The Old Mistress, weak and sick from all the opium she had used, had died of fright. Some of the servants had run away. Others had been taken by the bandits.

Cuckoo told Wang Lung that all the land, except the family's burial ground, was for sale. There were over 300 acres. That same day Wang Lung traded the glittering jewels for the land.

6 Wang Lung and Lotus

Now Wang Lung had more land than one man could take care of. So he added another room to his house, bought a donkey, and went to see his neighbor, Ching.

"Sell me your little piece of land, and leave your lonely house. Come into my house, and help me with my land," he said. Ching was glad to do this.

Wang Lung began to teach his sons how to work in the fields, and they helped him every day. But he would not allow O-lan to work in the fields, for he was no longer a poor man. That year he had to build yet another room onto his house to store his harvests.

O-lan worked in the house, making new clothes and shoes for everyone in the family. She made new coverings of flowered cloth for the beds. When all was finished, they were rich in clothing and in bedding as they had never been. And once more she gave birth—by herself.

On that day when Wang Lung came in from the fields, his father was standing at the door, smiling. "An egg with a double yolk this time!" he said. And so it was. Wang Lung went into the inner room. There on the bed were O-lan and two newborn babies, a boy and a girl.

The only sorrow that Wang Lung had at this time was that his elder girl was very slow. She did not speak or do anything that was right for her age. She only smiled her baby smile when she saw her father. He realized that if he had sold her, she would have been killed. "Little fool—my poor little fool," he groaned as he rocked her.

The years passed, and Wang Lung's fortune grew. Each year, Wang Lung hired more workers for his fields. Soon he had six men, and he built a new house behind his old one. He covered the house with tiles, and he and his family moved into it. The workers, with Ching at their head, lived in the old house in front.

It seemed that the few beans and seeds which had passed between these two men made them brothers. But Wang Lung, who was the younger, took the place of the elder. And Ching never completely forgot that he lived in another person's house.

By the fifth year, Wang Lung did not work much in the fields. He had to spend all his time selling his produce and taking care of other business. He was ashamed that he was not able to read contracts. And he could barely even write his own name. Once, he heard some clerks laughing at him, and he felt more ashamed than ever. He decided to send his elder son to school. Then his son could read and write for him.

By now the boy was 12 years old. When Wang Lung told him of his plan, the boy's eyes shone. "My father," he said, "I have wished for two years to go to school. But I did not dare ask for it." When the second son heard of it, he came crying to his father. He said that he, too, wanted to go to school. So Wang Lung sent both of them.

From the time they started school, they were no longer called Elder and Younger. After asking about the work of their father, the teacher named them Nung En and Nung Wen. The first word of each name meant "one whose wealth is from the earth."

After seven years of good harvests, flood waters came. But Wang Lung was not afraid, even though almost half of his land was a deep lake. Wang Lung had built his house on a hill. He had filled his store rooms with harvests, and they could easily survive a season of flood. But a man cannot sit all day and stare at a lake of water. Wang Lung began to grow bored.

He looked at O-lan and saw a dull and common creature. He saw once more that her features had no beauty. Her hands and feet were large and spreading. He said to her, "You look like the wife of a poor man. You don't look like the wife of a man who has land!"

It was the first time he had said such things to her. She looked at him, her mouth gaping open and showing her blackened teeth. Then she blushed and said, "Since the twins were born, I have not been well. There is a pain in my stomach."

He saw that she thought he was angry because she had not had a baby for more than seven years. But she had misunderstood. "Can't you buy a little oil for your hair? And those feet of yours—" He stopped. It seemed to him that the worst thing about her were those big feet.

At last she said in a whisper, "My mother did not bind them, since I was sold so young. But I will bind the younger girl's feet."

Wang Lung left the house because he was ashamed that he was angry with her. He walked to the town, thinking about O-lan on the way. He remembered that he could not have bought all his lands without the jewels O-lan had given him.

When he got to town, he was feeling restless. As he looked for something to do, he remembered that a new tea shop had opened. He had passed by it before, filled with horror at the thought of how money was spent there. Men gambled and spent money on evil women. But now, wishing to escape his guilt, he went in.

At first he did not speak at all. He just bought his tea, drank it, and looked around with wonder. The shop was a great hall, and the ceiling was decorated with gold. On the walls were pictures of women. Wang Lung thought that they were the women of dreams. He had never seen any like them on earth. The first day, he looked at the pictures, drank his tea quickly, and left.

But the flood waters held on to his land, and he kept going back to the tea shop. One evening, a woman tapped him on the shoulder. He turned around and saw that it was Cuckoo, the woman who had sold him the Hwang land. She told him that he could meet any of the women in the pictures. "Put silver in my hand, and I will place the one you choose before you."

Wang Lung looked at the pictures with a new interest. Up the stairway then, in the rooms above him, were these women. He looked at every painted face closely, and he finally chose the one he thought was most beautiful. But he said nothing to Cuckoo. He was too ashamed. He paid for his tea and went out quickly.

If the flood waters had gone down or if a child had fallen ill, Wang Lung would have had something to do. He might never have gone back to the tea shop. But in his own house, Wang Lung was bored and restless. One evening, he put on his good coat that O-lan had made for feast days. Without a word he left the house and went to the tea shop.

He was greeted by Cuckoo, whose job it was to get some customers for the women. When he told Cuckoo what he wanted, she took his silver and led him to an upstairs room. There sat a slender girl.

Wang Lung could not believe how beautiful she was. Her hands were small, and her long nails were stained the color of lotus buds, deep and rosy. Her little feet were in pink satin shoes no longer than a man's middle finger. Her figure was as slender as bamboo. She had a small pointed face and round eyes the shape of apricots. When she put her small hand on his arm, he began to tremble.

Wang Lung became sick with love for Lotus, as the girl was called. Every day he went to the tea shop, and he could not be with her enough. He was like a man dying of thirst who drinks salt water. Though it is water, it only makes him more thirsty. All that summer Wang Lung was in love with Lotus and could think of nothing else.

He could not even look at O-lan, the children, or his old father. As the days passed, he did what he could to please Lotus. When she laughed at his braid, he had it cut off. When O-lan saw what he had done, she said, "You have cut off your life!"

He began to bathe every day, using sweet-smelling soap. He stopped eating garlic, although he had always loved it. He was afraid the smell of it would offend Lotus. He had new clothes made, and he kept these clothes at the tea shop. He was ashamed to wear them in front of O-lan and the children. He began to spend a lot of money on Lotus, giving her gold pins and other gifts.

One day he stood before O-lan and asked, "Where are those pearls you had?"

Looking up from the edge of the pool where she was washing clothes, O-lan said, "I have them. I might have them made into earrings for our younger daughter when she is wed."

"Why should she wear pearls? Pearls are for pretty women! Give them to me!"

Then slowly O-lan reached inside her clothes and pulled out the small package. She gave it to him and watched as he unwrapped it. The pearls lay in his hand and caught the light of the sun, and he laughed.

But O-lan returned to the beating of his clothes. When her tears dropped slowly and heavily from her eyes, she did not wipe them away. She only kept beating her wooden stick on the clothes spread over the stone.

7 Lotus Moves In

It might have gone on forever like this until all the silver was spent. But then Wang Lung's uncle returned suddenly. He did not explain where he had been. He just stood there in the doorway in his ragged clothes, grinning at them as they ate breakfast. Wang Lung looked at him, surprised. He had forgotten that his uncle was alive, and it was like a dead man returning.

Wang Lung invited him in to eat, and the uncle helped himself freely to everything on the table. Then he said, as though it was his right, "Now I will sleep. I haven't slept for three days."

Wang Lung led his uncle to his father's bed, not knowing what else to do. When the uncle saw the good furniture and bedding in the room, he said, "Well, I heard you were rich, but I did not know you were as rich as this." Then he threw himself on the bed as if it were his own. He was asleep within moments.

Wang Lung was very upset, for he knew that his uncle would never leave. Not only that, but his wife and son would be moving in, too. Wang Lung had no choice but to let them, for that was the custom. As long as Wang Lung had money to spare, he had to take care of his family.

Three days after his uncle's family moved in, Wang Lung was still angry about it. O-lan said, "Stop being angry. This is something we must do." And Wang Lung knew that she was right. Then his thoughts turned more strongly than ever to Lotus. He said to himself, "When a man's house is full of wild dogs, he must seek peace elsewhere."

Now what O-lan and Wang Lung's father had not seen, his uncle's wife saw right away. "Your man is mad over another woman," she told O-lan. Wang Lung was trying to nap in his room when he overheard this. He was instantly wide awake and listened as she spoke.

Her voice went on, "I have seen it before. When a man buys new clothes and shoes and bathes every day, there is a new woman. Don't be surprised when he decides to bring her to this house to live. All men do so. My own husband would certainly do the same if he were rich enough!"

Until that moment, Wang Lung hadn't even thought of moving Lotus into his house. But now he saw a way to satisfy his longing for this girl he loved. He would buy her and bring her to his house. No other man could spend time with her again.

While the matter was being arranged, Wang Lung called his workers to him. He told them to build an addition to his house. He wanted another court behind the middle room. Around the court he wanted three rooms, one large and two small.

When the rooms were finished, he had bricks brought in. He had the workers add a good brick floor to the three rooms for Lotus. And he bought red cloth to hang at the doors for curtains. He bought furniture, including a large bed with flowered curtains around it. Then he had a little pool made in the center of the court. He lined it with tiles and bought five goldfish for it.

During all this time, he said nothing to his family except to scold them. One morning O-lan burst into tears and wept aloud. "I have given you sons," she moaned. "I have given you sons."

He was ashamed of himself, and so he stopped scolding her for little things. It was true that he had no reason to complain about his wife. There was no reason for him to have Lotus move in except that he wanted to.

One shining day toward the end of summer, Lotus came to his house. From afar Wang Lung saw her coming. She rode in a closed chair of bamboo carried on men's shoulders. When she arrived at the gate and stepped out of the chair, she kept her eyes lowered. She was leaning on Cuckoo, unable to walk by herself. It was part of

the arrangement that Cuckoo would also live there, as a servant to Lotus. As Lotus passed Wang Lung, she did not speak to him. She only whispered to Cuckoo, "Where is my apartment?"

Not long after that, Wang Lung dared to lift the red curtain and go into the court he had built for Lotus. Then he went into the darkened room where she was. He stayed with her the whole day.

All this time, O-lan had not come near the house. At dawn she had left with a hoe, her children, and some food. When night came, she returned with the children to the house. She said nothing to anyone. She went to the kitchen and made dinner as she always did. She helped the old man and the elder girl to eat. And then she ate a little. While Wang Lung still sat at the table dreaming, she got ready for bed. At last she went to her room and slept alone upon her bed.

Wang Lung spent every day with Lotus. All day she lay in the cool darkness of her room, eating fine foods and wearing green silk clothing.

It is not to be thought that the coming of Lotus and Cuckoo into Wang Lung's house caused no problems. More than one woman under one roof is never peaceful. The first thing he saw was that O-lan would have nothing to do with Cuckoo. This surprised him because he was prepared for O-lan to hate Lotus. But he had not expected that she would take out her anger on Cuckoo.

Of course, Lotus needed a servant since she could barely walk. No one would have expected O-lan to serve her. And the idea of his uncle's wife serving Lotus did not appeal to Wang Lung. He didn't want his uncle's wife peeping and prying into his business. So Cuckoo was the only choice.

Cuckoo tried to be friendly to O-lan, but O-lan would not even speak to her. She remembered how Cuckoo had always mistreated her when they were both slaves in the great house. Now that they were under the same roof again, O-lan didn't like it.

"It is a bitter thing in my own house," she said to Wang Lung. "And I have no mother's house to go back to." As she left the room, she felt for the door because her tears were blinding her.

Wang Lung was ashamed, but he said to himself, "Well, other men have done the same. I have been good enough to her. There are worse men than I. O-lan will just have to bear it."

But O-lan never had anything to do with Cuckoo. She would not even give her heated water to take to Lotus. When Wang Lung asked her to give Cuckoo hot water in the morning, she said, "No. I am not a slave of slaves in this house."

"But it is not for the servant. It is for her mistress," said Wang Lung.

O-lan said, "And to that one you gave my two pearls!" That was the only time O-lan ever said a thing about Lotus. She was too proud to ever mention her name or even complain about her.

Wang Lung soon had another kitchen built for Cuckoo and Lotus. He could see that O-lan would never share hers. He thought all his troubles were over at last. But he soon noticed that Cuckoo was buying very expensive foods. Some were foods he had never even heard of. Day after day, this food cost him a lot of money. But there was no one to whom he could complain. He began to notice that his love for Lotus was beginning to cool a bit.

There was yet more trouble for Wang Lung. One day he heard a shriek from Lotus in the inner court. The twins had been led to the inner court by his elder daughter, his poor fool. The younger children were, of course, curious about this lady who lived in the inner court. Lotus had complained many times about Wang Lung's children. But he had said to her, "They like to see a pretty face as much as their father does."

He had told them not to enter her courts, but sometimes they did so anyway. This day, the daughter had gone to Lotus's rooms with the twins. When she saw the bright silk clothing and the shining jade earrings on Lotus, she laughed aloud.

Lotus was frightened, and she screamed and shook her finger at the poor girl. Then she said, "I will not stay here if that idiot comes near me. I was not told that such a one lived here. If I had known, I never would have come!"

Then a deep anger awoke in Wang Lung, for he loved his children. He said, "You will not speak like that about my children." He was very mad that Lotus would say such things about his poor fool. For two days he would not go near Lotus, but instead played with his children. When he finally went back to Lotus, she tried to make it up to him. But he never loved her the same way again.

Finally the floods were gone, and it was time to work in the fields again. Wang Lung said, "Where is the hoe and where is the plow? And where is the seed for planting? Come, Ching, my friend. Call the men. I go out to the land!"

Wang Lung was healed of his sickness of love by the good dark earth of his fields. He worked hard and found joy in doing so. It seemed to Wang Lung that he had been away from the earth too long. Suddenly he could see everything that had to be done. He worked every morning and came in at noon for the meal O-lan had made. And when he went to Lotus smelling of garlic and cabbage, he laughed and cared nothing about it. Now he was full of health again and free of the sickness of his love.

So the two women took their place in his house. And Wang Lung felt proud when other men in the village talked with envy about Lotus. They knew that Wang Lung could afford to have her. And because he could afford her, he could have her with no shame. For such was the custom.

The men of the village looked at Wang Lung with more respect. He began to be seen as a leader. He was asked to settle arguments and to give advice. And Wang Lung was also proud of his sons who could read. He depended on his sons to read contracts for him. He was proud when they found things that had to be changed in the writing.

But one day Wang Lung noticed that his eldest son was acting like a young lord. He sometimes did not go to school, and instead acted in a lazy manner. Wang Lung was surprised, for he had never acted like that before. He had always been busy, up at dawn and working all day. He was secretly proud that his son did not have to work so hard.

He said to O-lan, "I cannot buy a slave for him. I will find a wife for him, and we will marry him early. We must do this right away."

Then he rose and went into the inner court.

8 O-lan's Illness

When Lotus saw that Wang Lung was thinking of other things than herself, she pouted. She said to him, "It's only been a year. Now you look at me but don't see me. If I had known this would happen, I would have stayed in the tea house."

Wang Lung then took her hand and kissed it. He said, "Well, a man can't always be thinking of the jewel he has sewn inside his coat. But if it were lost, he could not bear it. These days, I have been thinking about my eldest son. It is time for him to be married, but I do not know how to find a wife for him."

Lotus told Wang Lung that she knew a grain merchant who used to come to the tea house. He had a daughter who looked something like Lotus, small and fine. He was a good man, always kind to the girls in the tea house. She wasn't sure where he worked, so she called Cuckoo into the room.

Cuckoo told Wang Lung that the grain merchant, named Liu, had his shop in the Street of the Stone Bridge. Wang Lung struck his hands together in delight and said, "That is where I sell my grain. It is a good sign. It would be good luck to wed my son to the daughter of the man who buys my grain."

Cuckoo smelled money in it as a rat smells cheese. She said, "I can make all the arrangements for you." She smiled as she thought of the matchmaker's fee in her hand.

But Wang Lung was not quite ready to make a decision yet. "I must think about this for a few days," he said. The next morning, though, his mind was made up for him. His eldest son came home after the sun was up. He had been out all night, drinking and having a good time with his uncle. When he saw the state his son was in, Wang Lung knew he had to arrange the marriage soon.

He went to Cuckoo and said, "Go to the grain merchant and arrange the matter." Then he went to his son's room and sat beside him as he slept. As he smelled the liquor on his son's breath, he became angry with his uncle. He thought, "I have taken in an ungrateful nest of snakes. Now they have bitten me!"

He found his uncle leaning over a table eating his breakfast. He shouted at him, "Get out of my house, you and your family! From this moment on, there will be no more rice for any of you. I will burn the house down rather than have you in it. You have no gratitude, and you are ruining my son!"

But his uncle sat where he was and kept eating. He said, "Drive me out if you dare." Then the uncle opened his coat and showed what was against its lining. It was a false beard of red hair and a length of red cloth. Wang Lung stared at these things, and then he understood his real position.

The red beard and the red cloth meant he was a member of a band of robbers. These robbers thought nothing of burning down a man's house and carrying his women away. In all his years of good harvests, Wang Lung had never been robbed. Now he understood why. Wang Lung had thought that he was protected by Heaven. Now he knew that he would be safe only as long as he fed his uncle's family.

As if he didn't have enough trouble, Cuckoo came back from the grain merchant with bad news. The grain merchant agreed that his daughter would marry Wang Lung's son. But she was only 14 years old, and the marriage would have to wait for three years. Wang Lung was worried as he thought of three more years of the boy's idleness. He said to O-lan, "Let us arrange marriages for the other children as soon as possible. I cannot go through this three more times!"

Wang Lung's troubles were too deep for him. So, as he usually did when this happened, he

took a hoe and went out to his fields. As he passed through the outer court, he saw his elder girl sitting there smiling. She was twisting a bit of cloth through her fingers and smoothing it out. This simple act seemed to keep her busy. Wang Lung thought, "That poor fool brings me more comfort than all the others put together."

Wang Lung went out to his land every day. One day, a small cloud came out of the South. It did not move as clouds blown by the wind do. The men of the village watched it and talked of it. Fear came over them, for they knew that it was a cloud of locusts. Wang Lung forgot all his other troubles.

To fight the locusts, who would eat all his crops, he worked day and night. He called his workers together. They set fire to some fields of wheat. They dug wide moats around other fields and ran water into them. Some of the locusts fell into the fires or into the water. By the time the cloud of locusts moved on, Wang Lung had managed to save some of his crops. There was wheat to reap, and his young rice beds were spared.

The locusts had forced him to think of nothing but his land. He was healed of his other troubles. He thought, "My uncle is older than I, and he will die soon. My son will get through the next three years until he is wed. And my life will go on."

One day, after Wang Lung had said to himself that peace was in his house, his eldest son came to him. He said, "Father, I would like to go to a great school in the South. The old teacher in this town has no more to teach me."

"You know enough for these parts. I say you cannot go," said Wang Lung. He looked at his son. His skin was smooth and golden. His hands were soft and fine as a woman's. Then he looked at himself. He was thick and stained with earth. He looked more like his son's servant than his father. This thought made him angry at his son. He shouted, "Go out into the fields. Rub a little good earth on yourself so you'll look like a man. Work a little for the rice you eat!"

That evening, when Wang Lung was sitting beside Lotus, she said, "Your son is so unhappy. He wants to go away."

Wang Lung said, "How do you know that? I do not want him in these rooms at his age."

Lotus told Wang Lung that she had heard it from Cuckoo. And Cuckoo said, "Anyone can see that your son is unhappy."

But Wang Lung said that he would not spend his money foolishly by sending his son away. For many days, nothing more was said about it. Then one evening O-lan came softly into his room. She said to him, "Your eldest son goes too often into the inner courts. When you are away, he goes. It would be better to send him away, even to the South."

Wang Lung did not believe O-lan at first. But then he remembered that Lotus had known that his son wanted to go away. How had she known? His son had also stopped talking about going away. He seemed more content now. Why was he so happy? Wang Lung decided to find out for himself.

The next morning, he said loudly that he was going to town and would be back late. When he had gone halfway, he turned around and went back home. He stood at the curtain that hung in the door to the inner court. He heard a man's voice. It was the voice of his own son. Full of an anger he had never known before, he went outside and got a piece of bamboo from the grove. Then he went back softly and suddenly tore aside the curtain.

There was his son, standing in the court, looking down at Lotus. Lotus sat on a small stool at the edge of the pool. They were talking and laughing. Wang Lung fell on his son, beating him with the bamboo. When Lotus screamed and pulled at his arm, he beat her too, until she ran to her room. When he was finished beating his son, he said, "Pack your things. Tomorrow, you will go south. Do not come home until I send for you."

When the eldest son was gone, Wang Lung felt better. He then decided to take his second son out of school and have him learn a trade. He arranged for the boy to work as an apprentice to Liu, the grain merchant. While he was talking to Liu about this, he also talked of arranging another marriage between their families. They spoke about betrothing Wang Lung's ten-year-old daughter to Liu's ten-year-old son. The final decision would have to wait. This was not a thing that could be discussed further face to face.

Later that day, Wang Lung noticed that his ten-year-old daughter had been crying. When he asked her why, she said, "My mother has been binding my feet. Each day, she ties the cloth more tightly. It hurts so much that I cannot sleep at night."

"I have not heard you crying before," he said.

"No," she said. "My mother said I was not to cry in front of you. She said you are too kind and weak for pain. If you saw me crying, you would tell her not to bind my feet. Then my husband would not love me, just as you do not love her."

When Wang Lung heard this, he felt as if he were being stabbed. He thought of how O-lan had been the first woman he had ever known. He thought of how she had been a faithful helper beside him. He thought of what the child had said, and he was sad. With all her dimness, O-lan had seen the truth in him.

Wang Lung was proud because he had three sons. One was a scholar, one was a merchant, and one was a farmer. Now he began to think about the woman who had given him these sons. He thought of her with a strange kind of sorrow. He saw that she had grown thin, and her skin was dry. He remembered that sometimes in the morning he heard her groaning as she lit the oven. He wondered why she was moving more slowly these days. And he wondered at the strange swelling in her belly, even though she was not with child.

One day, he saw her face turn gray with some inner pain. He asked her what it was, and she said, "It is only the old pain in my stomach." Seeing for the first time how sick she was, he told her to go to bed. He went to get a doctor.

After the doctor had examined O-lan, he told Wang Lung what was wrong. "The spleen is enlarged. The liver is diseased. She has a large tumor in her womb, and her stomach has holes in it. Her heart is barely moving."

Not wanting to tell Wang Lung that his wife would soon die, the doctor set a very high price to cure her. For ten pieces of silver, he could prescribe a broth that might ease her pain. But it would take 5,000 pieces of silver to guarantee her recovery. Wang Lung looked at the doctor in sad silence. He would have to sell all his land to get that much silver. He knew that the doctor was trying to tell him that O-lan was dying.

He went out with the doctor and paid him the ten pieces of silver. When the doctor was gone, Wang Lung went into the dark kitchen. He turned his face to the blackened wall, and he wept.

9 Changes in the Family

O-lan lay dying for many months. For the first time, Wang Lung and his children knew what she had been in the house. She had provided comfort for them all, and they had not known it. Now the house was messy, and the meals were not cooked well. The old man missed the way O-lan had always waited on him.

All during the winter, Wang Lung did not take care of his land. Instead, he sat by O-lan's bed. If she was cold, he lit a fire to keep her warm. Each time she would say, "It's too expensive."

One day, when she said this, he could not bear it. He said, "Don't say that! I would sell all my land if it could heal you."

She smiled and said, "I would not let you. For I must die sometime anyway. But the land is still there." But he would not talk about her death, and he left the room whenever she spoke of it.

Even so, he knew that she must die, and one day he went into town to a coffin-maker's shop. He ordered a good black coffin made from heavy and hard wood. The coffin-maker offered him a better deal if he bought two, so Wang Lung ordered one for his father. When Wang Lung told

O-lan what he had done, she was pleased. Wang Lung had provided well for her death.

One day O-lan asked for Cuckoo. Wang Lung was surprised, but he called Cuckoo right away. When Cuckoo got there, O-lan sat up in bed and spoke plainly to her. She said, "You may have lived in the courts of the Old Lord. You may have been thought of as beautiful. But I have been a man's wife, and I have given him sons. And you are still a slave." Then she said to Wang Lung, "After I am dead, do not let that one or her mistress come into my room and touch my things. If they do, I will send my spirit back for a curse."

Then one day O-lan was suddenly better, as a candle flickers brightly at its end. She sat up in bed and asked for some tea. She said to Wang Lung, "I have been thinking. I want to see my daughter-in-law, who is betrothed to our eldest son. I want her to stay with me, so I can get to know her." So Wang Lung arranged for the girl to come to their house, and she took care of O-lan for three days.

Then O-lan said to Wang Lung, "There is another thing. I want my son to come home. I must die, but I want him to wed this maid first. Then I may die easily." So Wang Lung sent for his eldest son. And Liu, the grain merchant, agreed to let his daughter marry a year earlier than they had planned.

The wedding took place three days later. Lotus and Cuckoo and the wife of Wang Lung's uncle helped the girl get ready. They painted her with powder and with red paint. They rubbed fragrant almond oil into her skin. With a brush they painted her eyebrows in two long slender lines. They set upon her head the bride's crown and beaded veil. And on her tiny feet they put embroidered shoes.

When at last she was ready, she was led into the middle room, where Wang Lung's son was waiting. He was dressed in a red robe and a black jacket. Wang Lung thought to himself that if only O-lan had been well, it would have been a happy day. After the ceremony, there was feasting. O-lan could hear the noise and laughter from her bed. She was happy that her son was married and would soon be having sons of his own.

After the guests had left, Wang Lung sat by O-lan's bed, holding her hand. She slept on and off for a few hours. Finally, she opened her eyes and stared at him, as if she wondered who he was. Suddenly her head dropped off the round pillow, and she was dead.

The next day, Wang Lung went to a fortune teller to find out a lucky day for her burial. He found a good day three months ahead. Then he rented a space in the temple for O-lan's coffin to

rest until burial. He could not sleep in the room where O-lan had died. So he moved into the inner court where Lotus lived. He told his son and his wife to move into O-lan's room.

Then, as if death could not leave the house, Wang Lung's father died, too. O-lan and Wang Lung's father were buried on the same day, on a hill under a date tree. A wall had been built around the graves. There was enough space inside the walls for the whole family, even for the sons' sons. Dead and alive, the family of Wang Lung would rest upon their own land.

As he stood over O-lan's grave, he remembered a day when she washed his clothes at the pool. He wished he had not taken the pearls from her that day. From then on, he would never allow Lotus to wear them again.

Walking home from the graves, he thought, "There is buried the first good half of my life and more. It is as if half of me were buried there. Now it is a different life in my house." And suddenly he wept, drying his eyes with the back of his hand as a child does.

That year, flood waters again covered the land. There were no harvests of any kind, and everywhere people were starving. Many people went south, and many others died of hunger. Some joined the robber bands that were roaming the land.

The waters did not go down in time for the next year's planting. So Wang Lung knew that there would be another year of no harvests. He was very careful about the amount of food used in the household. Each day, he gave his daughter-in-law just enough for that day. But Wang Lung was not as poor as he wanted others to think. He had silver hidden in many places. He knew that many people hated him because he still had food to eat. So he kept his gates barred, and he let no one in that he did not know.

He knew that if it were not for his uncle's power, he would have been robbed long ago. So he tried to be nice to his uncle and his uncle's family. Now the uncle, his wife, and his son could see that Wang Lung was afraid. They began to demand this and that. They complained about the food. One day, Wang Lung overheard the wife and son talking to his uncle. They said that he should demand silver from Wang Lung in exchange for his protection.

First the uncle asked Wang Lung for silver so his wife could buy a new coat. Next it was for a new pipe for himself. This went on and on. Wang Lung resented his uncle's demands, but he had no choice. As long as the uncle was happy, Wang Lung was safe from the Redbeards.

One day, Wang Lung's eldest son said, "You care more for them than you do for us. Maybe we should set up our house elsewhere." But when Wang Lung explained the truth to his son, his son's eyes opened wide. Then he became very angry. He suggested that they drown the uncle, the uncle's wife, and their son in the flood waters.

Wang Lung refused to do this for several reasons. First, he could never kill anyone. And second, what if he did and the other robbers heard about it? No, his uncle had to stay alive.

Then he said, "If only we could keep them here but make them harmless!"

Then Wang Lung's eldest son had an idea. He said, "Let us buy them opium to enjoy. It might cost a lot. But it will be cheaper than giving them silver whenever they ask for it." After thinking about this for a few days, Wang Lung agreed that it was a good plan.

One day soon after that, Wang Lung said to his uncle, "Here is a little better tobacco for you." From then on, he made sure there was plenty of opium lying around. He pretended to smoke some himself. But he only took the pipe to his room and let it sit there cold. And he would not let his sons and Lotus touch the opium. But he gave it to his uncle, his uncle's wife, and their son. It was worth the silver it cost because it brought Wang Lung peace.

As winter ended, the flood waters began to go down. Then Wang Lung's eldest son announced that a grandson was on the way. Wang Lung sent Ching to town to buy fish and good food for his son's wife. "Eat," he told her. "Make my grandson strong." All during the spring, Wang Lung thought with happiness about the grandson that was coming.

As spring grew into summer, people started coming back from the South. They had to build new houses, for the old ones had been washed away. Many came to Wang Lung to borrow money. He loaned it at high interest. When they needed oxen, plows, and seed but could borrow no more money, some sold part of their fields. From these people, Wang Lung bought more land.

Some of the people would not sell their land. When they had no money, they sold their daughters. Many of them came to Wang Lung because he was a man of good heart. Wang Lung, thinking about his growing family, bought five slaves in one day. When his grandchildren were born, each would have a slave.

A few days later, a man came with a small girl of seven years, wanting to sell her. Wang Lung thought she was too small and weak, but Lotus wanted her. "She is so pretty," said Lotus. So Wang Lung bought the child for 20 pieces of silver, and she lived in the inner courts with Lotus. Her name was Pear Blossom.

It finally seemed to Wang Lung that he could have peace in his house. But it was not to be. There was trouble between his eldest son and his uncle's son. Wang Lung's son thought that the uncle's son was looking at the new slaves in an evil way. He didn't tell his father that the uncle's son also looked at Lotus. He only told his father what he thought the best plan was.

"The old great house of the Hwangs is for sale. We should buy it and move into it. We can leave your uncle and his family here. And we will finally have peace," said the eldest son.

This seemed like a good idea to Wang Lung. He had never forgotten that once he had felt shame in that house. Now, he had it in his power to sit on the same seat where the Old Mistress had sat. His second son said, "I could wed and have my wife there also. We would all be under one roof, as a great family is."

The more Wang Lung thought of it, the more he liked the idea. Finally, he went to look at the house to see if he wanted to buy it. As he was walking through the rooms, he came to the raised platform where the Old Mistress had sat. He sat down in the same place. Then he struck the table with his hand and said, "This house I will have!

10 The Family Grows

These days, once Wang Lung had decided something, he could not do it fast enough. He told his eldest son to arrange for the move as soon as possible. On moving day, Lotus and Cuckoo and their slaves and goods were moved first. Then Wang Lung's eldest son and his wife and their servants and slaves followed. But Wang Lung did not move on that day. He decided to stay at the old house for a while. He promised to move into the new house before his grandson was born. Meanwhile, he would try to find a wife for his second son.

Wang Lung's uncle, wife, and son moved into the inner courts where Lotus had been. Wang Lung did not mind, for he could see that his uncle would not live much longer. As soon as the uncle died, Wang Lung's duties toward that part of the family would be ended. No one would blame him if he kicked the son out then.

With Ching's help, a bride was found for Wang Lung's second son. When the arrangements were made, Wang Lung was glad. He thought, "Now there is but one more son to wed. Then I will be able to rest."

By now, Ching was getting old. He was too tired to manage the workers and all the land. Wang Lung did not want to work very hard, so he rented out some of his land. Because he owned the land, he would receive half of the harvests.

One day, his uncle's son came to ask Wang Lung for money so he could join the war in the North. Wang Lung was glad to give it, so he could get rid of the boy.

Finally, there was peace in Wang Lung's life. He spent more and more time at the new house. Soon his grandson would be born. He bought silk and satin for his family to wear. And he bought good blue and black cotton for the slaves. No one in his house had to wear ragged clothing. And Wang Lung started to eat fancy foods and sleep late.

One morning, he heard the groans of a woman, and he knew that his grandson was about to be born. "But what if it is a girl!" Wang Lung thought suddenly. This was the first time he had thought about this. He burned some incense in front of a statue of the goddess of mercy, asking for a boy. Then he burned some more incense at his small temple in the fields.

That evening, he found out that he had a grandson. As Wang Lung thought about how happy he was, he remembered O-lan. He remembered how she had had her babies silently, with no help from anyone. And here was this one, his son's wife, who cried like a child in her pains.

Not long after this day, a worker came running from the harvest fields. He brought the news that Ching had been working too hard and now lay dying. By the time Wang Lung got to Ching's side, the man was almost gone. His face was spotted with blood, and his half-opened eyes were blind. He could not even speak. He lay there panting until he died.

Wang Lung wept as he had not wept when his own father died. He ordered a coffin of the best kind and ordered his family to mourn for three days. He wanted to bury Ching inside the wall where his father and O-lan were buried. But his sons said, "Should our mother and grandfather lie with a servant? And must we also, when we die?" So Wang Lung had Ching buried near the entrance instead of inside the walls. And he told his sons that when he died, he wanted to lie nearest to Ching.

After Ching died, Wang Lung went less and less to see his lands. It hurt him to go there without Ching. So he rented out all the land that he could, but he would never sell it. He had one of his workers stay in the country house to care for his uncle and his wife. And he brought his youngest son and his poor fool with him to the big house in town.

Now at last, Wang Lung thought he could enjoy his life in peace. But his eldest son wanted to improve the house. He had many ideas for redecorating and buying new furniture. To keep peace, Wang Lung told his son to go ahead. The young man bought carved tables and chairs. He bought curtains of red silk to hang in the doorways. He bought vases large and small. And he bought scrolls to hang on the walls. Finally, the second son came to Wang Lung to complain.

"Father," he said, "my brother is spending too much money. All this money lent out at 20 percent would have brought in many pounds of silver. What is the use of all these pools and lilies and goldfish?"

"Well, it is all for your wedding," said Wang Lung, hoping this would bring peace.

Then the young man said, "It is an odd thing for the wedding to cost ten times as much as the bride. He is spending our inheritance. That money should be divided among us when you are dead. Instead, he is spending it just to impress other people."

After thinking about it for a short time, Wang Lung told the elder son to stop spending so much. The son answered, "Well, I will stop spending money on the house. But there is one more thing. My youngest brother should not be growing up ignorant. He weeps at night, for he does not wish to be a farmer. You have prepared him for nothing else. He should be taught something."

Now Wang Lung had never thought to ask his youngest son what he wanted to do with his life. He sent for his youngest son right away. As the boy stood before him, Wang Lung saw how handsome he was. He said, "Your eldest brother says you wish to learn to read. He says you do not wish to work on the land. Is this true?"

The boy answered only one word, "Yes."

At first Wang Lung was angry, but as soon as his anger passed, he called his eldest son to him. He said, "Hire a teacher for the third son. Let him do as he likes. Just don't trouble me about it. Leave me in peace."

And he called his second son to him. He said, "Since I am not to have a son on the land, you will have more duties. From now on, you will collect the rents on the land and take care of all the silver."

The second son was pleased, for this meant that the money would pass through his hands first. He could complain to his father if too much were spent in the house. The second son was very careful about money, even the money that was spent on his own wedding. Indeed, his elder brother was ashamed of the way the second son was so careful with money.

It seemed that none of the sons was really happy. The eldest wanted to spend more, the second wanted to spend less, and the youngest wanted to learn more. The only person in the whole house who seemed really happy was Wang Lung's grandson. This small one had known only the life of the great house. Here lived his mother, his father, his grandfather, and more servants than he would ever need. Wang Lung took great delight in playing with the child. Only in this way did Wang Lung find peace.

Over the next five years, Wang Lung had four more grandsons and three granddaughters. Each child had a slave. Each year Wang Lung saw more children and slaves in the courts, and he was pleased and happy.

The winter of the fifth year was very cold. A constant icy wind blew from the northeast. Fur coats could not even keep a person warm. In every room of the great house they burned fires to heat the air.

Now Wang Lung's uncle and his wife had been smoking opium for many years. They were by this time as thin as two old dry sticks. There was no warmth in them. Wang Lung heard that his uncle couldn't even sit up in bed anymore. When he went to see his uncle, he could tell that the old man would not live many more hours.

So he bought two coffins of wood, which were good enough but not too good. He had the coffins brought into the room where his uncle lay so he could see them. Then he could die in peace, knowing there was a place for his bones. "You are a better son to me than my own," said the uncle.

Not long after that, the uncle died, and Wang Lung had him buried near his father. Then he moved his uncle's wife into a room in the great house. There she lay on her bed all day, sucking her opium pipe. When Wang Lung looked at her, he thought of the Old Mistress in the fallen House of Hwang. His uncle's wife was just as yellow, silent, and shriveled.

All his life, Wang Lung had heard of war here and there. But he had never seen one up close. To him war was a thing like earth and sky and water. He didn't know what it was, but only that it was. One day, his second son came home from the market for his noon rice. He said to his father, "The price of grain has gone up suddenly. The war, which is coming closer every day, will make the price go up even higher. As the armies come nearer to us, we can sell for a good price."

Wang Lung remembered that once he had been afraid of war. That was when he might have been seized against his will. But now he was old and rich, and the rich need not fear anything.

One day, long ranks of gray-coated men filled the streets of the town. Wang Lung looked closely and saw that each man was wild and tough-looking. And each one had a weapon of some kind with a knife sticking out of the end. Suddenly, one of the men shouted at him, "Hello there, my old father's nephew!"

Wang Lung saw the son of his uncle, dressed like the others. But his face was wilder than the rest. The nephew called out to the other soldiers, "We can stop here, my friends. This is a rich man, and he is my relative!"

Before Wang Lung could even move, the men ran past him into his courts. The next few months were a nightmare for Wang Lung and his family. The soldiers took over the whole place, eating what they wanted and making a lot of noise. Wang Lung could do nothing about it. His second son had told him that the soldiers would kill anyone for the smallest reason. Then finally the war called, and the men left, leaving behind the damage they had done to the courts.

11 Wang Lung's Last Years

When the soldiers were gone, Wang Lung and his two elder sons for once agreed on something. They decided that every trace of the soldiers must be wiped away. They hired workers to mend the broken furniture and clean the courts. They planted more trees and cleaned out the goldfish pools. Within a year, the place was fresh and flowering again.

One day, the wife of Wang Lung's uncle died in her sleep. The slave who had been taking care of her put the old woman in her coffin. Then she asked Wang Lung to find a husband for her. So Wang Lung did this.

Now, he felt that his life was complete. In the very house where he had once come to get O-lan, he was now arranging marriages. By now, he was close to 65 years old. His grandsons were growing, and his third son was old enough to be married.

But still there was no peace for Wang Lung. He was having some trouble with Lotus. For some reason, Lotus had a strange idea in her head. She thought that Wang Lung wanted her slave,

Pear Blossom, to be his own slave.

Now nothing could have been further from the truth. But once Lotus mentioned it, Wang Lung started to think about Pear Blossom. She was a beautiful girl. She would make any man happy.

Then he thought of his third son, who had talked about joining the army. The boy had listened to the soldiers when they had been at the great house. He had heard their tales of battles, and he had read books about war. His head was full of the glory he thought he would find in war.

Then Wang Lung asked his son why he wanted to be a soldier. The boy said, "There is going to be a revolution. Soon our land will be free!" Wang Lung had no idea what his son was talking about. In Wang Lung's mind, the land was already free.

"I do not know what freedom you want more than you already have," he said to his son. Wang Lung did not want his son to go to war. He thought that if he found a wife for him, he would be happy to stay home. When he mentioned this to the son, the young man was not interested. He said, "A woman is not the answer to everything, as it is to my eldest brother."

Then Wang Lung thought that maybe his son would be happy with a mistress instead of a wife. So he asked his son if there was a slave that interested him. The only slave the young man liked was Pear Blossom, so Wang Lung spoke to her about the idea.

But she said, "Young men are not kind. They are only cruel and fierce. I like old men. They are so kind and gentle." And her small childish voice made Wang Lung feel very protective. From that day on, Pear Blossom was his constant companion.

Wang Lung got another slave for Lotus, to take Pear Blossom's place. Now Wang Lung's only problem was his youngest son. He still wanted to be a soldier, and Wang Lung was still against the idea. One night, his youngest son left suddenly without saying good-bye. Where he had gone, no one knew.

Almost as suddenly as his son's leaving, Wang Lung began to feel old. He was very fond of Pear Blossom, and she served him faithfully and patiently. He was always kind to her, and his feelings for her were as a father for a daughter.

For his sake, Pear Blossom was even kind to his poor fool. This was a great comfort to him. One day, he told Pear Blossom what had long been on his mind. Wang Lung had always worried about what would happen to his poor fool when he was dead. No one but himself cared whether she lived or died. So he had bought a little bit of poison at the medicine shop. He planned to put some in her food when he saw that his own death was near. But still he dreaded this more than he dreaded dying. So he called Pear Blossom to him.

He said, "You are the only one to whom I can leave this poor fool after I die. She will live on and on after me because her mind has no troubles of its own. I know that no one will think about feeding her or bringing her in out of the rain. Perhaps she will even be sent out to wander on the street. Now here is a gate of safety for her in this packet. When I am dead, you are to mix it in her rice and let her eat it. Then she may follow me where I am. And so I shall be at peace."

Pear Blossom would not take the poison from Wang Lung. She said, "I cannot even kill an insect. How could I take this life? No, my lord, but I will take care of your fool because you have been kinder to me than anyone in my whole life."

Wang Lung could have wept for what she said, but he asked her to take the packet anyway. He said, "Even you must die one day. Save it until that time." Pear Blossom took the poison and said no more. Wang Lung trusted her and was comforted.

Then Wang Lung began to age more quickly. He lived alone in his courts, except for Pear Blossom and his fool. Sometimes he looked at

Pear Blossom and said, "It is too quiet a life for you, my child."

But she always answered, "It is quiet and safe. You are kind, and that is all I want from any man."

One day he asked her, "What happened to you that made you so fearful of men?"

He saw great terror in her eyes, and she covered them. Then she whispered, "I hate every man but you. I hate even my father who sold me."

She would say nothing more. He wondered whether something had once happened to her that she would not tell him. He wondered if Lotus had told her evil things about men. But he sighed and stopped thinking about it. Above all, he wished only to sit in his court near Pear Blossom and his fool.

So Wang Lung sat, and his old age came on him day by day and year by year. One day, he asked one of his sons, "How many grandchildren do I have now?"

"Your sons have eleven sons and eight daughters," he was told.

Then Wang Lung sat a little while and looked at the children. "That one looks like his great-grandfather. And there is a small merchant Liu. And there is myself when I was young," he thought.

One time he asked Cuckoo, "Has anyone ever heard from that youngest son of mine?"

And Cuckoo answered, "He has not written. But now and then, someone comes from the South with news about him. It is said that he is a high-ranking officer in the army."

And so the years continued to pass. The only thing that continued to matter to Wang Lung was his love for his land. He had gone away from it and he had set up his house in a town. He was rich, but his roots were in his land. When spring came each year, he went out onto the land. He could no longer hold a plow or do anything on the land, but he had to go anyway. He would sleep in the old earthen house and in the old bed where O-lan had died.

One day in the late spring, he wandered to the place on the hill were he had buried his dead. He stood looking at the graves and remembering each person. They were more clear to him now than the sons who lived in his own house. As he thought of his dead, he thought, "Well, I shall be the next."

Then he went inside the little wall and he saw the place where he would lie. He would be below his father and his uncle and above Ching and not far from O-lan. And he stared at the bit of earth where he was to lie. He saw himself in it and back in his own land forever. Then he thought, "I must see about getting a coffin."

So he went to his eldest son and told him what he had been thinking. "Do not speak like that, father!" said his son. "But since you wish it, I will do as you say."

His son bought a coffin made out of a wood that was as lasting as iron. Wang Lung had the coffin brought into his room. He looked at it every day. Then suddenly he decided to move back to the earthen house. So he, Pear Blossom, his poor fool, and a few servants went to the old house. He also had the coffin moved there.

Spring and summer passed into autumn. Wang Lung thought about nothing except his food and his drink and his land. But he didn't think of planting anything or of the harvests. He thought of the land itself. Sometimes he would gather some of the earth up in his hand and hold it. It seemed full of life. And he was content, thinking of how the kind earth waited for him to come to it.

One day, when his sons were visiting, he heard them talking. He heard only the words "sell the land."

"What, evil sons, sell the land?" He choked and would have fallen, but they caught him. He began to weep, and they tried to comfort him.

"No, no, we will never sell the land," they said.

"It is the end of a family when they begin to sell the land," said Wang Lung. "Out of the land we came and into it we must go. If you will hold your land, you can live. No one can rob you of land."

And the old man let his tears dry on his face. He bent over and took up a handful of the soil. He held it and said, "If you sell the land, it is the end."

And his two sons held him, one on either side. And they said over and over, "Rest easy, father, rest easy. The land will not be sold."

But over the old man's head, they looked at each other and smiled.